BARD
OF THE
DEAL

BARD
OF THE
DEAL

THE POETRY OF
DONALD TRUMP

HART SEELY

HARPER

NEW YORK • LONDON • TORONTO • SYDNEY

HARPER

BARD OF THE DEAL. Copyright © 2015 by Hart Seely. All rights reserved. Printed in the United States of America. No part of this book may be used or reproduced in any manner whatsoever without written permission except in the case of brief quotations embodied in critical articles and reviews. For information, address HarperCollins Publishers, 195 Broadway, New York, NY 10007.

HarperCollins books may be purchased for educational, business, or sales promotional use. For information, please e-mail the Special Markets Department at SPsales@harpercollins.com.

FIRST EDITION

Library of Congress Cataloging-in-Publication Data has been applied for.

ISBN 978-0-06-246516-0

15 16 17 18 19   OV/RRD   10 9 8 7 6 5 4 3 2 1

CONTENTS

FOREWORD

Donald Trump—the Businessman—has built magnificent palaces and golf courses, even better than Pebble Beach, while attaching his name to the smoothest vodkas and tastiest steaks.

Donald Trump—the Entertainer—has penned bestsellers, regaled Larry King, and hosted a top-rated TV show, *The Apprentice*, succeeding where even the likes of Martha Stewart failed.

Donald Trump—the Man—has dated supermodels, graced the cover of *Playboy*, raised world-class children, and even bested Merv Griffin in a duel of wits.

But it is Donald Trump—the Poet—who has stared wide-eyed into the jaws of hell to bring back the meaning of life.

> We're here. And we live our
> sixty, seventy or eighty years,
> and we're gone.

> You win, you win, and
> in the end, it doesn't mean

a hell of a lot.

But it is something to do.

Ever since the summer of 2015, when Donald John Trump announced his candidacy for president, the nation and the world have been captivated by his stream-of-consciousness, teleprompter-free speeches. At rallies and news conferences, supporters hear a long-awaited call for an upgrade of the U.S. population. Critics hear racism, sexism, and an out-of-control ego. Either way, listen carefully, and you will hear—as 18,000 fans did one night in Texas—the anguished cry of the Poet.

IT'S DEPRESSING

You know, it's depressing.
Isn't it depressing?
You know, we're together.
We love each other.
But it's like depressing,
If you think about it,
Because it doesn't end.
I could stand up here
All night long,
I could tell you stories.
They are all depressing.

SEPTEMBER 14, 2015

Welcome to the first-ever treasury of Trumpian verse—poems culled from a towering pile of speeches, interviews, utterances, and tweets that has risen over the last thirty years. This collection answers one of the great mysteries of modern times: What is the secret to Donald Trump's astonishing success?

In these pages, you will see that it is not wild ambition or savage greed, or the Wharton School, or a patch of unearthly hair. What separates "The Donald" from the rest of us is one amazing, God-given talent:

Whenever Trump opens his mouth, poems—like winged dollar signs in a Scrooge McDuck cartoon—flutter out upon the wind.

On a regular basis, Trump's spontaneous emissions address and *undress* the fundamental realities of reality—as if they were the realities of reality TV. Consider his lyrical discourses on:

GOD

Who has read *The Art of the Deal?*
Yeah! Most people, most everybody!
I joking say, but I mean it:
The Bible tops it, by a long way.

DEATH

Sad. Horrible Statement.
I hate to say it, but I say it,

You know, because it's true.

Life is what you do while you wait to die.

PROCREATION

Frankly, I wouldn't mind
If there were an anti-Viagra,
Something with
The opposite effect.

I'm not bragging.

PERFECTION

We have a chef who makes
The greatest meat loaf in the world.
It's so great I told him
To put it on the menu.

In 2015, the Poet unveiled his most enduring meta-phorical image yet: A magnificent "wall" that would protect America from rapists. To anyone who follows big league poetry, Trump was clearly sending out a broadside toward his twentieth-century predecessor Robert Frost. It was Frost who once wrote, *"Before I built a wall I'd ask to know/ What I was walling in or walling out."* With his customary flair, Trump responds, *"We would make it very good looking/ It would be as good as a wall's got to be."* End of debate. We won't be hearing from Frost again—or for that matter, Elizabeth "Kill all the men!" Barrett Browning. *(Have you seen her pictures? Woof.)*

Today, the "Billion-Dollar Bard" bestrides the world's literary scene like it's the bottle-strewn boardwalk of Atlantic City. Trump's powerful verses—written to be shouted at lefties and lowlifes—have changed the way Americans see not only their government but their next-door neighbor. His poetry embodies the difference between classic—and *classy!* And the Poet's message is being received.

Yes! We want good deals!

Yes! We want to make America rich!

Yes! We want so many victories that they are coming out of our eyes, our nose, our ears, our whatever!

These poems come from Trump's published utterances—taken verbatim, without a word altered. The lone changes involve punctuation, capitalization, and use of the most critical tool known to poetry: the carriage return key.

So, sit back, grill a Trump Steak, pour a tall glass of Trump Vodka, and go "Trumpster diving" for some billion-dollar stanzas, straight from the Bard of the Deal. As the Poet himself might say, this stuff is like very, very, *very* good.

PART ONE

TRUMP STATE OF MIND

LIFE

You do what you do.
I mean,
It is what it is.

September 11, 2015
NBC *TONIGHT SHOW WITH
JIMMY FALLON*

ACHIEVING THE LOOK

I get up, take a shower
And wash my hair.
Then I read the newspapers
And watch the news on television,
And slowly the hair dries . . .
It takes about an hour.

I don't use a blow-dryer.
Once it's dry, I comb it.
Once I have it the way I like it,
Even though nobody else likes it,
I spray it and . . .
It's good for the day.

October 2004
PLAYBOY

CLASSROOM SIZE

I've seen a lot.
I understand life.
I understand how to make money.
And if I can impart some
of what I've learned,
whether you call it "wisdom" or not,
to a large group of people,
I like it.
And as far as I'm concerned,

The larger the crowd, the better.

March 9, 2006
CNN *LARRY KING LIVE*

WHEN TO QUIT

How do you know when to give up?
I usually tough it out
longer than most people would
in a similar situation,
which is why I often succeed,
where others have failed.

I also know that sometimes
you have to throw in the towel.
Maybe you failed
but you probably learned
something valuable.
Chalk it up to experience,
don't take it personally,
and go find your next challenge!

2008
TRUMP Never Give Up:
How I Turned My Biggest
Challenges into Success
WITH CO-POET
MEREDITH McIVER

THE ENTIRETY OF LIFE

We're here. And we live our
sixty, seventy, or eighty years,
and we're gone.

You win, you win, and
in the end, it doesn't mean
a hell of a lot.

But it is something to do.

March 1990
PLAYBOY

MY HAIR

I have beautiful hair.
It's not that bad.
And it is my hair.
Is it my hair?
It is.
It is, actually.
People don't know that.
I proved that, you know,
In Alabama.

It was really hot.
It was rainy.
I took off my hat
And everybody said
"It is really his hair!"
It's weird.
I don't have
To do that tonight.
Sort of nice.

August 25, 2015
Trump rally
DUBUQUE, IOWA

HOW'S IT GOING . . . REALLY?

Small talk can be
One of the best ways
To educate yourself.
Rarely does a day go by
In which I don't have
Five to ten conversations
That change the way
I see the world.

2004
Trump: Think Like a Billionaire
WITH CO-POET
MEREDITH McIVER

KANYE

KANYE WEST!
You know what?
I'll never say bad about him!
You know why?
Because he loves Trump!

He loves Trump!
He goes around saying,
"TRUMP IS MY ALL-TIME HERO!"
He says it to everybody!
So, KANYE WEST?
I LOVE HIM!

September 3, 2015
Press briefing
NEW YORK CITY

IF THEY BUILD A WALL

If there's a wall
in front of you,

You have to
go through it.

You can never,
ever give up.

November 24, 2004
CNN *LARRY KING LIVE*

RULES OF LEADERSHIP

Your behavior should be at all times
Attuned to the matter at hand.

Grandstanding or talking
Just to hear yourself talk

Are counterproductive.

2004
Trump: Think Like a Billionaire
WITH CO-POET
MEREDITH McIVER

SUCCESS IN THE MEDIA

It's a simple formula
in entertainment and television:
If you get good ratings,
if you get good ratings,

and these aren't good,
these are MONSTER,

Then you're going
to be on all the time,
even if you have
nothing to say.

September 14, 2015
Trump rally
DALLAS, TEXAS

FRAGRANCE GUARANTEE

Any man who wears this fragrance
Can have any woman
—*Or man*—
That you want.

It's your choice!

December 1, 2004
TRUMP: THE FRAGRANCE,
LAUNCH PARTY

NOT GAY

You know, if I were gay,

which is, perhaps,
a well-known story
that I'm not,

I would admit that I'm gay.

October 9, 2006
CNN *LARRY KING LIVE*

RICH MAN, POOR MAN

I think a poor person can be
Just as happy as a rich person
Depending on that person's
Health and family, the basics once again.
But I couldn't be happy if I were poor.
I'm just too spoiled.

Hopefully, I won't ever have to deal with it.

August 28, 1994
NEW YORK TIMES

LOST STORY

I had a story recently.
It was the best story,
one of the best stories
I've ever had.

But in the second paragraph,
He says, "But he wears
the worst hair piece
of any human being I've ever . . ."

And it's *my* hair.

And so I can't even
show the story.

December 15, 2014
REMARKS TO THE ECONOMIC
CLUB OF WASHINGTON, D.C.

I GREW UP IN NEW YORK

A town with different races,
Religions,
And peoples.

I have learned to work with
My brother man.

December 8, 1999
LOS ANGELES DAILY NEWS

A WELL-EDUCATED BLACK

If I were starting off today,
I would love to be
A well-educated black,

Because I believe
They do have
An actual advantage.

September 5, 1989
The R.A.C.E.: Racial Attitude
Consciousness Exam
NBC NEWS

LIVING IN THE MOMENT

You have moments of meanness.
You have moments of love.
You have moments of, like . . .

    Everything.

                March 9, 2006
                CNN *LARRY KING LIVE*

HOW TO LOVE YOUR JOB

Always pretend that you're working for yourself.
You'll do a wonderful job in that case.
It's simple, but it works.
If you're finding that you don't love your job,
Or that you're not doing a good job,
Demand a meeting with your boss immediately.
If the situation doesn't improve, fire yourself.

2004
Trump: Think Like a Billionaire
WITH CO-POET
MEREDITH McIVER

POWERS AND ABILITIES

Quite often,
I'll be talking to someone,
And I'll know what
They're going to say
Before they say it.

After the first three words
Are out of their mouth,
I can tell what
The next forty
Are going to be.

2004
Trump: Think Like a Billionaire
WITH CO-POET
MEREDITH McIVER

REVENGE THERAPY

It's very therapeutic, Larry.
You're a revenge person.
I know you very well.

You're a revenge person.
It's a very therapeutic way
of taking care of your own head.

October 15, 2007
CNN *LARRY KING LIVE*

GOOD DEEDS

They'd much rather see me,
you know, beating someone up
than being nice to somebody.
You know, it fits the image
better for them.

And I think that's fine.
It doesn't matter.
But I love to help people.
I do. I love helping people.
There's nothing better.

There's nothing that
makes me feel better.

May 17, 2005
CNN *LARRY KING LIVE*

THE GAP

In New York, you have the best of lives,
the worst of lives, and some in between.
You look at the wealthiest people in the world
living in one section, and literally, within eyesight,
you have people that are not doing so well.
Sometimes, people ask me for money.
And, usually, these are people, who
are suffering some very serious problems,
but sometimes they will ask . . . and sometimes I'll help.

April 6, 1998
New York magazine
"DONALD TRUMP: EGO
BUILDER"

DYNASTY

There has always been
a display of wealth
and always will be,
until the Depression comes,
which it always does.

And let me tell you,
a display is a good thing.
It shows people
that you can be successful.
It can show you a way of life.
Dynasty did it on TV.

March 1990
PLAYBOY

GLITZ

I don't use glitz in all cases.
And in my residential buildings,
I sometimes use flash,
Which is a level below glitz.

March 1990
PLAYBOY

GRAY SHOES

Do you know the driver that
came over today had gray shoes on?

Yeah, the motherfucker
had gray shoes.

He looked like some
goddamn Puerto Rican.

He looked like somebody
we picked up from Spanish Harlem.

Nobody—fucking nobody—
wears gray shoes for me.

1991
*Trumped! The Inside Story of the
Real Donald Trump—His Cunning
Rise & Spectacular Fall*
BY JOHN R. O'DONNELL
(WITH JAMES RUTHERFORD)

ASKING FOR FORGIVENESS

When we go into church—and
when I drink my little wine—which
is about the only wine I drink—
and have my little cracker—
I guess that is a form of
asking for forgiveness.
I do that as often as possible because

I feel cleansed, OK?

July 19, 2015
IOWA FAMILY LEADERSHIP
SUMMIT

OH, THE THINGS YOU'LL TEACH!
(A SEUSSIAN SCREECH)

I love it!
I love teaching!
I love teaching people
   how to make it in life.

   And, you know, *HEY!*
    And that's not said
   in a braggadocious way!

March 9, 2006
CNN *LARRY KING LIVE*

GOD, IN HEAVEN

For the record,
I don't think I'm God.

I believe in God.

If God ever wanted
An apartment in Trump Tower,
I would immediately offer
My best luxury suite . . .

At a very special price.

2004
Trump: Think Like a Billionaire
WITH CO-POET
MEREDITH McIVER

MERRY CHRISTMAS, ASSHOLES!

You can't even use the word "Christmas" anymore!
Macy's doesn't use the word "Christmas," I mean,
You can't even use the word "Christmas" anymore!
And, you know, with me, it is going to stop.
IT IS GOING TO STOP!

September 3, 2015
THE ECONOMIST

HAIR

It is raining, now,
At least you know
It IS my hair . . .

Because

It's raining out here.
If this WASN'T my hair.
Believe me . . .

I would not be out here.

June 30, 2015
CNN *ANDERSON COOPER 360°*

NEPOTISM

I like nepotism.
I think, you know,

A lot of people say,
"Oh! Nepotism!"

Usually, these are
people without children.

October 9, 2006
CNN *LARRY KING LIVE*

FAMILY

There is nothing
To compare with family

If they happen
To be competent.

1987

TRUMP: THE ART OF THE DEAL

OH, THE CHILDREN YOU'LL RAISE (A SEUSSIAN PRAISE)

Children is a beautiful thing to do.

So we're
having a baby.

If I have more, that's OK, *too*!

March 9, 2006
CNN *LARRY KING LIVE*

THE GAME

It's to many people's advantage to like me.
Would the phone stop ringing?
Would these people kissing ass disappear?
If things were not going well?
I enjoy testing friendship.

Everything in life, to me, is a psychological game.

March 1990
PLAYBOY

IF HE KNEW ME . . .

If he knew me,
I think he'd like me.

If he doesn't know me,
perhaps he wouldn't.

But if he knew me,
I think he'd probably like me.

He's a little bit of a
different kind of a pope.

September 20, 2015
NBC *MEET THE PRESS*

PLAN AHEAD

See what I do?
All this bullshit?
Know what?

After shaking
five thousand hands,
I think I'll go wash mine.

May 19, 1997
THE NEW YORKER

BAD REVIEWS

I.

The show has gotten great reviews.
I've gotten great reviews,
Everything, gotten great reviews,
Except for one thing,
My hair gets bad reviews.

II.

I take a shower, I wash it,
I then comb it and set it
And I spray it and it's good for the day,
But I'm getting killed on my hair.

February 27, 2004
CNN *LARRY KING LIVE*

THE BIGGEST BOOK

Who has read *The Art of the Deal*?
Yeah! Most people, most everybody!
I joking say, but I mean it:
The Bible tops it, by a long way.

I say that. I say that.
Said it the first time in Iowa.
People liked that. But it's true.
Nothing tops the Bible.

August 29, 2015
National Federation of Republican
Assemblies
NASHVILLE, TENNESSEE

CHALLENGE TO OBAMA

I love
that he
was golfing,

Because
I own
twelve
great courses.

I'd love
to play
him for the
presidency.

March 16, 2011
FOX NEWS CHANNEL *YOUR
WORLD WITH NEIL CAVUTO*

THE CAT IN THE RAIN
(A SEUSSIAN REFRAIN)

You know, if it rains,
I'll take off my hat
And I'll prove,
Once and for all, THAT . . .
    It is mine, OK?

August 21, 2015
SPEECH IN MOBILE, ALABAMA

LIFE

Life—this is sad.
No politician would say this,
So you know I'm not going to be a politician.

Life is what you do while you're waiting to die.

Sad. Horrible statement.
I hate to say it, but I say it,
You know, because it's true.

Life is what you do while you wait to die.

Have fun.

March 21, 2004
CNN *LATE EDITION WITH
WOLF BLITZER*

PART TWO

THE WHATEVER FORCE

THE WHATEVER FORCE

The reason people like what I'm saying
is because they want to put that energy,

    whatever the hell
    kind of energy it is,
    I don't know
    if it's screwed up,
    if it's good,
    if it's genius,
    if it's,
    whatever it is . . .

I know how to do things.

                  August 21, 2015
                  Trump rally
                  MOBILE, ALABAMA

SOME GOOD THINGS ABOUT ME

I've never smoked a cigarette in my life.
I've never had a drink,
Never had a joint, never had any drugs,
Never even had a cup of coffee. So,
Those are some good things about me.

I probably have some bad things about me, too.

May 11, 2011
ROLLING STONE

WHAT I DO IS I DO DEALS

What I do is I do deals.
I deal.
I have tremendous energy,
tremendous,

to a point where it's almost
ridiculous.

September 14, 2015
Trump rally
DALLAS, TEXAS

WHY I FIGHT

My main purpose in life
is to keep winning.
And the reason
for that is simple:

If I don't win,
I don't get to
fight the next battle.

1990
Trump: Surviving at the Top
WITH CO-POET
CHARLES LEERHSEN

THE NAME

I was born with a name
that just sort of worked for me.
It worked on buildings.
It's concise; it's a winning card.

And I was able to take that name
And do very important things with it.
If my name was Joe Blow,
It just wouldn't have played.

April 6, 1998
New York magazine
"DONALD TRUMP:
EGO BUILDER"

SMART TRUMP

I had an uncle
Who went to MIT
Who is a top professor.
Dr. John Trump.
A genius.
It's my blood.
I'm smart.
Great marks.
Like, really smart.

June 30, 2015
CNN *ANDERSON COOPER 360°*

SELF

Hey, I've got my name
on half the major buildings
in New York.

I went to the Wharton
School of Finance, which is
The No. 1 school.

I'm intelligent.
Some people
Would say I'm

Very, very, very intelligent.

April 3, 2000
FORTUNE

HIGH EDUCATION

My family is terrific.
I mean, they really are.
Now, they're highly educated.
My family is highly educated.
I'm highly educated,
which until *The Apprentice*,
most people didn't know.
They thought I was a barbarian.
But I'm highly educated.

February 27, 2004
CNN *LARRY KING LIVE*

AYE-YI-YI!
(A SEUSSIAN CRY)

AYE-YI-YI!

They see me walking down the street
and they go . . .

"HEY, HEY, HEY!"

But then, I'm good at that stuff,
you know?

August 29, 2015
National Federation of Republican
Assemblies
NASHVILLE, TENNESSEE

ON BEAUTY

Part of the beauty
Of me

Is that I'm very
Rich.

March 17, 2011
ABC *GOOD MORNING AMERICA*

MIGHTY SWORD

Viagra is wonderful
If you need it.
If you have medical issues . . .
If you've had surgery . . .
I've just never needed it.

Frankly, I wouldn't mind
If there were an anti-Viagra,
Something with
The opposite effect.
I'm not bragging.

October 2004
PLAYBOY

KING OF THE HOOD

Did you know my name
Is in more black songs
Than any other name in hip-hop?
Black entertainers love Donald Trump.

Russell Simmons told me that.
Russell said, "You're in more hip-hop songs
Than any other person,
Like five of them lately."

That's a great honor.

October 2004
PLAYBOY

THE HONOR

It's a great honor. You know,
they're doing a two-hour movie on me
on national network television.
And so I'm honored in one way.
In another way, I want it to be accurate.

So, if it's not accurate, I will sue.

May 17, 2005
CNN *LARRY KING LIVE*

SMITH, JONES, ROSENBERG

The name "TRUMP" was a good name.
I have a lot of friends who are named

    Smith.
    Jones.
    Rosenberg.

Names that won't work, necessarily.
TRUMP is a great name.

It's the winning card.

2005
No Such Thing as Over-Exposure:
Inside the Life and Celebrity of
Donald Trump
BY ROBERT SLATER

WORKING MY ASS OFF

These other guys,
they go around,
They make a speech
In front of twenty-one people.
Nobody cares.

They make the—
They read the same speech.
They have teleprompters.
I say we should outlaw teleprompters
for anybody, right?

For anybody,
For anybody running for president.
You know how easy that would be?
Instead of this?
I'm working my ass off!

August 25, 2015
Speech in Dubuque, Iowa
CNN *ANDERSON COOPER 360°*

MY FANTASY

I would love President Bush
to call me and say,
"Go over and negotiate peace
between the Palestinians and Israel."
I would love to do that.

That's one thing that I would
probably like doing more
than building great towers
all over the place
because I really believe,

With the right intermediary,
the right mediator,
the right negotiator,
you could go over
and really do a job.

November 24, 2004
CNN *LARRY KING SHOW*

BRAINADOCIOUS

I do know what I'm doing.
and I don't say that
in a braggadocious way.

You people are looking
for somebody that knows
what he's doing.

Whatever it is.

August 21, 2015
SPEECH IN MOBILE, ALABAMA

BEAUTIFUL PHRASE

Every time I walk outside,
Somebody says it.
And the funny thing is,
Everybody thinks
I'm hearing it for the first time.
"YOU'RE FIRED!"
I get it literally 100 times a day.

Little kids come up to me and say,
"Mr. Trump, YOU'RE FIRED!"
And then run away, laughing.
It became a mania.
"YOU'RE FIRED!" hats and T-shirts
Sell like hotcakes.
It's a beautiful phrase.

October 2004
PLAYBOY

THE VISION

I've made a tremendous amount of money.
I've had tremendous success.
And I don't say that braggingly.
That's the kind of thinking we need in this country.
I mean, whatever it is.

August 29, 2015
National Federation of
Republican Assemblies
NASHVILLE, TENNESSEE

ON SAYING, "YOU'RE FIRED!"

It's not like, *"Oh, gee, please!*
Give me another chance!"
It doesn't work that way.

It's so succinct. It's so
beautiful in its finiteness.
And it's just—it's over.

It's just over.

> November 24, 2004
> CNN *LARRY KING LIVE*

THE ELEMENTS

So many different elements
running through *The Apprentice*
that are amazing.

There's love. There's hate.
There is potential
Racism.

March 21, 2004
CNN *LATE EDITION WITH
WOLF BLITZER*

VERY WELL HAIKU

Believe me, folks. We
Will do very, very well,
Very, very well.

June 16, 2015
Announcement of presidential candidacy
NEW YORK CITY

ON BEING WORTH TEN BILLION DOLLARS

The number is actually much higher
Than anybody ever knew.
And I'm not saying that to brag.

I'm only saying that because,
That is the kind of thinking
our country needs.

July 11, 2015
PHOENIX, ARIZONA

INVINCIBLE

I'm the one!
The most militaristic person!
I would build a military . . .
   So strong!
   So powerful!
   So incredible!
Nobody would ever use it.

August 25, 2015
Speech in Dubuque, Iowa
CNN *ANDERSON COOPER 360°*

BAD TIMING

Look at this!
Can you believe it?
I was supposed to be
On page one!

But because of Lady Di,
I ended up
On page three!
THIS IS CRAZY!

2005
No Such Thing as Over-Exposure:
Inside the Life and Celebrity of
Donald Trump
BY ROBERT SLATER

THE PLEASANT WAY TO SAY IT

Usually, if I fire somebody who's bad,
I'll tell them how great they are.
Because I don't want to hurt people's feelings.
I'm actually a much nicer person
than people think, you know.

I'll tell them they're great.
They're unbelievable,
They have an unbelievable future,
And that I'm holding them back
By having them in my company.

May 17, 2005
CNN *LARRY KING LIVE*

RESPECT

I have respect for Mitt Romney.
I don't know him,
But I have respect for him.

The fact that my net worth is
Many, many, many times greater,
I'm not knocking him.

April 18, 2011
ABC NEWS INTERVIEW WITH
GEORGE STEPHANOPOULOS

OH, THERE'S NOT ENOUGH TIME!
(A SEUSSIAN RHYME)

I don't have very much time!
I just don't have very much time!

There's nothing I can do
About what I do!

Other than stopping,

AND I JUST DON'T WANT TO!

May 19, 1997
THE NEW YORKER

DENYING THE MEAT

We have a chef who makes
The greatest meat loaf in the world.
It's so great I told him
To put it on the menu.

So whenever we have it,
Half the people order it.
But then afterward,
If you ask them what they ate . . .

They always deny it.

May 19, 1997
THE NEW YORKER

I DO GREAT

I do great with Tea Party,
I do great with conservatives,
I do great with moderates,
I do great with evangelicals,
I do great with everybody.

September 3, 2015
THE ECONOMIST

ON SECOND THOUGHT

OH, MY GOD, NO!
They're going to kill me in the press!
They'll kill me!
I can't do anything like that.
The Tour de Trump?
Nah, they'll destroy me!

    But . . .

Isn't that what it's all about?
Yeah. They'll kill me!
But I love it!
I love it!
I love the idea!
LET'S DO THIS!

1991
Trumped! The Inside Story of the
Real Donald Trump—His Cunning
Rise & Spectacular Fall
BY JOHN R. O'DONNELL
(WITH JAMES RUTHERFORD)

TWITTER

I have millions of followers, millions.
I don't do press releases anymore.
If I want a press release, I just put it on Twitter
And I've got a press release.

It's so great. It's like owning
The New York Times
Without the losses.
No, it is.

May 27, 2014
NATIONAL PRESS CLUB

WILD CNN HAIKU

CNN has been
Wild about the whole Trump thing,
Whatever that is.

August 19, 2015
HOLLYWOOD REPORTER

WHO NEEDS CAMPAIGNING?

I haven't even started campaigning yet.
Now, maybe when
I start campaigning, I'll do worse.

Perhaps I shouldn't campaign at all.
I'll just, you know,
I'll ride it right into the White House.

October 8, 1999
CNN *LARRY KING LIVE*

FREE TO BE ME

I can pivot any way.
I can be a very elegant,
Highly refined person.

I can be a very
Politically correct person,
Where I would never, ever

Say anything that's even
Slightly over the edge, or . . .
I can be who I want to be.

August 19, 2015
HOLLYWOOD REPORTER

THE CALLING

Let's cut to the chase.

Yes, I am considering a run
for the Presidency
of the United States.

The reason has
nothing to do with vanity.

2000
TRUMP: The America We Deserve
WITH CO-POET DAVE SHIFLETT

PART THREE

THE HORRIBLE ONES

THE HORRIBLE ONES

Some of them are not nice.
Some of them are
HORRIBLE HUMAN BEINGS.

OK?
But they're the greatest in the world.

Do we want nice people?
Or do we want these
HORRIBLE HUMAN BEINGS

To negotiate for us?
Horrible!
I want horrible!
I WANT THE HORRIBLE!

August 14, 2015
Hopkinton State Fair
CONTOOCOOK,
NEW HAMPSHIRE

ON CRITICIZING

It's best to avoid criticizing anyone.
Compliments work better,
And sometimes silence is
The best form of criticism available.

I've known people who have said
Bad things to and about me
Who cannot take criticism themselves.
Most people are one-way streets.

And it's better not to spend your time
Dodging head-on traffic.
If you stay silent, people will eventually
Make fools of themselves without your help.

2004
Trump: Think Like a Billionaire
WITH CO-POET
MEREDITH McIVER

BEAUTY AND THE BEAST

So you have beauty
And then you have Rosie,
The Beast.

You have Beauty and the Beast.
So it works well.
And then you have Trump.

October 28, 2006
CNN *ANDERSON COOPER 360°*

SCUM

You're all jerkoffs.
I've never had so much
incompetent shit working for me.

First of all, you hired scum.
I got scum working for me here.
Walt was in charge, and he hired scum.

1991

*Trumped! The Inside Story of the
Real Donald Trump—His Cunning
Rise & Spectacular Fall*
BY JOHN R. O'DONNELL
(WITH JAMES RUTHERFORD)

THE MONEY COUNTER

i don't think he knows what
the fuck he's doing my
accountants up in new york
are always complaining about
him he's not responsive and
isn't it funny

i've got black accountants
at trump castle and at
trump plaza black guys
counting my money
i hate it

the only kind of people
i want counting my money
are short guys that wear
yarmulkes every day those
are the kind of people
i want counting my money
nobody else

besides that i've got to
tell you something else
i think that the guy is lazy.

and it's probably not his fault
because laziness is a trait
in blacks. it really is
i believe that

1991
*Trumped! The Inside Story of the
Real Donald Trump—His Cunning
Rise & Spectacular Fall*
BY JOHN R. O'DONNELL
(WITH JAMES RUTHERFORD)

NABISCO NABISCO

Nabisco. Nabisco!
Oreos! Right?
Oreos! I love Oreos!

I'll never eat them again. OK?
I'll never eat them again.
No . . . Nabisco.

August 21, 2015
SPEECH IN MOBILE, ALABAMA

THE PRESS

They don't want to give it straight,
Because the press are liars.

They're terrible people.
They're terrible people.
Terrible.

Not all of them, but many.

July 11, 2015
PHOENIX, ARIZONA

SCHMUCK HAIKU

You have me saying
These things, even though they're true,
I sound like a schmuck.

May 19, 1997
THE NEW YORKER

PUNDITS

They get paid a half a million dollars a year
To sit there and make jerks out of themselves, right?
Call them pundits.

Some are great.
Some are really incompetent.

I could say the ones,
But they're starting to get nicer to me,
So I think I can't.

August 21, 2015

SPEECH IN MOBILE, ALABAMA

THE GUTLESS SHALL PAY
FOR THEIR GUTLESSNESS

They're gutless; they're all gutless.
I have to sue Univision. Univision.
My poor Miss Universe people,
These beautiful women,
(Some are girls, but . . .)
Beautiful women,
And I get dropped.

Think of it. You have these
Magnificent women,
Who worked all their life
To be in the Miss USA contest, and the Miss—
And two weeks before the contest,
NBC and Univision dropped,
Because they thought my tone
Was a little bit strong.
And it turned out I was right.
So here's the good news.
I sued them both.

August 21, 2015
SPEECH IN MOBILE, ALABAMA

I GOT SCREWED OUT OF AN EMMY

Everybody thought I was gonna win it.
In fact, when they
announced the winner,
I stood up before the winner was announced.

And I started walking for the Emmy.
And then they announced
the most boring show on television,
The Amazing Race. Piece of crap.

January 19, 2015
NBC *CELEBRITY APPRENTICE*

CONTRACTORS

They can just rip you off if
You don't know what you're doing.
And there is nobody smarter
Than a contractor who
Can't read or write.

They're smarter than Wharton.

May 27, 2014
NATIONAL PRESS CLUB

CAPTURED McCAIN

He is a war hero . . .
He is a war hero
BECAUSE HE WAS CAPTURED.
I like people
Who WEREN'T captured . . .
    OK?

I hate to tell you . . .
He is a war hero
BECAUSE HE WAS CAPTURED . . .
    OK?

July 18, 2015
CNN *ANDERSON COOPER 360°*

HERO

John McCain's a great guy,
a tremendous guy!
I've known him for a long time.
and I'm with him.

And I'm with him,
based on the fact that
I have great knowledge
of John McCain.

September 17, 2008
CNN *LARRY KING LIVE*

LOSERS HAIKU

They were all great, smart,
Attractive people, but not
One of them is me.

October 2004
PLAYBOY

THE CARRIER

A guy walked into my office two weeks ago.
He shook my hand, hugged me,
Sat down and said,
"I have the worst flu I've ever had!"

The guy looked like he was dying,
And he'd just shaken my hand.
I said, "Why did you shake my hand?"
People don't have a clue.

It's disgusting.

October 2004
PLAYBOY

WHEN ROSIE CAME TO MY WEDDING

She ate like a pig.
And, I mean, seriously,
the wedding cake was, was—
It was like missing in action.
I couldn't stand there.
I didn't like it.

But a particular woman
wanted her at the wedding.
(Marla.) I think they were friendly
or something. And so I said,
what's Rosie O'Donnell doing here?
She was at my wedding.

October 15, 2007
CNN *LARRY KING LIVE*

DECLARATION

The phrase that
All men are created equal
Is a wonderful phrase,

But unfortunately
it doesn't work that way.

All men are not created equal.
Some are born with a genius and
Some are born without.

Now, you need that. If you don't have that,
You can forget it.

> March 21, 2004
> CNN *LATE EDITION WITH*
> *WOLF BLITZER*

PAT BUCHANAN

Look, he's a Hitler lover.
I guess he's an anti-Semite.
He doesn't like the blacks,
He doesn't like the gays.

It's just incredible that anybody
Could embrace this guy, and maybe
He'll get four or five percent
Of the vote. And it'll be a

Really staunch right-wing wacko vote.
I'm not even sure if it's right. It's just a wacko vote.

October 26, 1999
NBC *MEET THE PRESS*

CONDOLEEZZA WAVES

A lovely woman,
But she never makes a deal.
She doesn't make deals,
She waves.
She gets off the plane,
She waves.

She sits down with some dictator—
Forty-five-degree angle,
They do the camera shot.
She waves again.
She gets back on the plane,
She waves . . .

March 16, 2007
CNN *LATE EDITION WITH
WOLF BLITZER*

ROSIE, AGAIN

She got up in front of wonderful, young women
the other day at the Waldorf-Astoria.
She grabbed her crotch and she said,

    "Eat me."

Now, she was referring to me.

    "Eat me."

Now, there can be no more disgusting thing
For me to think of.

            April 25, 2007
            CNN *LARRY KING LIVE*

THE MOST HORRIBLE HUMAN
BEINGS ON EARTH

I have the smartest, toughest,
Meanest, in many cases,
The most horrible human beings on Earth.

I know them all. They're killers.
They're negotiators.
Some are nice people.

Very few.

August 21, 2015
SPEECH IN MOBILE, ALABAMA

PART FOUR

WOMEN, GOOD AND BAD

WOMEN, GOOD AND BAD

I don't think all women are gold diggers.

There's nothing more beautiful to me
Than a woman; I love and respect them.
I've known a lot of really good women
And have had amazing relationships
Over the years; but as with men . . .

There are good ones and bad ones.

October 2004
PLAYBOY

WONDERFUL WOMEN!

Women are TREMENDOUS!
I find women to be—
I mean women,
I've had such an amazing relationship
With women in business.
They are amazing executives.
They are KILLERS!
Now, when I say that about a man—
It's very sad . . .
If you say that about a man,
it's considered a great honor.
It's also a great honor
When you say it about a woman
Because—and that's the way it was meant.
They are PHENOMENAL!

August 9, 2015
ABC *THIS WEEK WITH*
GEORGE STEPHANOPOULOS

TWO POEMS ABOUT A BREAST PUMP

I.
What happened is,
    In the middle of everything,
    It wasn't breast-*feed*,
    You used the word "breast-feed."
    It was breast *pump*.
    She wanted to *pump* in front of me.

II.
I've never seen anything like it.
She wanted to breast-*pump* in front of me.
And I may have said "That's disgusting,"
I may have said something else.
I thought it was terrible.
She is a horrible person.

July 29, 2015
CNN *ANDERSON COOPER 360°*

CHERISH IS THE WORD
I USE TO DESCRIBE

I will be great on
Women's health issues.
I cherish women.

And I will be great on
Women's health issues.
Believe me.

August 11, 2015
News conference
BIRCH RUN, MICHIGAN

COMPANY

You really want
To know what I
Consider ideal company?

A total piece of ass!

April 26, 2011
The New Yorker
"BEST WISHES, DONALD"

TO MY BELOVED . . .

I say to Melania:

"You're beautiful.
I love you.
You're the greatest ever.
Unbelievable.
I can't live without you.
By the way,
Sign the prenup, OK?"

It's not exactly
the most romantic thing
in the world.

October 21, 2007
CNN *LARRY KING LIVE*

DISTRACTIONS

It is hard to stay married,
Because there is so much

    Diversity,
    Tension,
    Excitement,

And lots of other things.

April 6, 1998
New York magazine
"DONALD TRUMP:
EGO BUILDER"

STRIVING TO BE ON TOP

I'm a romantic guy.

If there isn't any romance in my life,
Then I don't have much incentive
To be the best that I can be.
That's one reason I love women.

They're great motivators.

2004
Trump: Think Like a Billionaire
WITH CO-POET
MEREDITH McIVER

A LAW OF PUBLICITY

You know, it really doesn't matter what
They write as long as you've got
A young and beautiful piece of ass.

But, she's got to be young and beautiful.

May 1991
ESQUIRE

LOVERS IN NEW YORK

People treat me with great respect,
and, in some cases, love.
They try to hug; they touch;
they do other things.

Not only are the people
in New York exciting,
but I think you have many of the
most beautiful people in New York.
I think you have
the most beautiful women
in the world in New York, too,
and for somebody like me,

That's not such a bad thing.

April 6, 1998
New York magazine
"DONALD TRUMP:
EGO BUILDER"

THE VICIOUS

I was attacked viciously
By those women,
Of course, it's very hard for them
To attack me on looks,
Because I'm so good-looking.
But I was attacked very viciously
By those women.

August 9, 2015
NBC *MEET THE PRESS*

LARRY'S WEAKNESS

They were chosen for their brain,
but they happen to be attractive. I mean,
the women, some of the women,
happen to be very attractive.

And they have used their sexuality
to win certain tasks, as we call them.
And, hey, that's part of life, I guess.
In real life, that happens, too.

I've known it. I've seen it happen.
It's actually happened to me
a couple of times. Larry, it's
happened to you many times.

February 27, 2004
CNN *LARRY KING LIVE*

WOMEN HAIKU

I have seen women
Manipulate men with just
A twitch of their eye.

1997

*TRUMP: THE ART OF THE
COMEBACK*

CLINTON'S MISTAKE

He handled the Monica situation
disgracefully; it's sad, because
he would go down as a great president,
if he had not had this scandal.

People would have been more
forgiving, if he'd had an affair
with a really beautiful woman
of sophistication.

Kennedy and Marilyn Monroe
were on a different level.

September 19, 1999
New York Times
MAUREEN DOWD COLUMN

LADIES AND THE TRAMPS

Women are much tougher
And more calculating than men.
I relate better to women.
I go out with the most beautiful women in the world.

Certain guys tell me they want
Women of substance,
Not beautiful models.
It just means they can't get beautiful models.

September 19, 1999
New York Times
MAUREEN DOWD COLUMN

WOMEN

I had two divorces.
And they were very good women.
And I always say about that—
They were excellent women.

Terrific women.
But you know what?
I work so hard and so long
That it's almost unfair to women.

April 18, 2011
ABC *THIS WEEK WITH*
GEORGE STEPHANOPOULOS

GOOD WIVES

I have had—actually,
I have a great marriage.
I have a great wife now.
And I—my two wives were very good.

June 28, 2015
CNN *STATE OF THE UNION*

A COMPARISON OF
BRET MICHAELS AND
MELANIA TRUMP

I saw him without a shirt
And he looked good.

Not as good as she looks
Without a shirt,

But he looked good.

April 28, 2010
CNN *LARRY KING LIVE*

A CRITICAL ASSESSMENT
OF ACTRESS HALLE BERRY,
USING THE STANDARDIZED
10-POINT SCALE

From the midsection
to the shoulders:
She's a ten.

The face is:
A solid eight.

And the legs are:
Maybe a little bit less.

August 8, 2015
New York Times
Maureen Dowd column
VIA *THE HOWARD STERN SHOW*

ONLY A DEVIANT

I have nothing against Megyn Kelly.
But she asked me a very, very nasty question.

And in the middle of her questioning,
I brought up a statement: "Rosie O'Donnell!"

And the entire place—it was the biggest
combination of laughter and applause!

The place went crazy! Interrupted her question.
It . . . It obviously shook her up a little bit.

But she was very angry, you could see it.
And I made the statement:

"Blood was falling from her eyes."
And then I said, "Blood was flowing from wherever."
     That—and I just—when I said that,
     I wanted to just get onto the—I didn't say anything.

     I was, excuse me, George. I was referring to
     Nose, ears . . . They're very common statements.

And only a deviant would think of what people said. Some people said only a deviant.

August 9, 2015
ABC This Week
TELEPHONE INTERVIEW

PART FIVE

MY AMIGOS

AND OTHER FOREIGNERS

MY AMIGOS

I love Mexico.
I love the Mexican people.
I have thousands of Mexican people

That have worked for me
Over the years,
And even to this day.

I mean, I love the Hispanics.
The spirit.
I love them.

August 25, 2015
Trump rally
DUBUQUE, IOWA

MEXICANS

They are not sending their best.
They are not sending you.
They are not sending you.
They are sending people
That have lots of problems.

And they are bringing
Those problems with us.
They are bringing drugs,
They are bringing crimes,
They're rapists.

And some, I assume, are good.

June 16, 2015
Announcement of presidential candidacy
NEW YORK CITY

THE TRUMP WALL

The Trump wall,
that would be a beautiful wall.
That's why I have to
make it beautiful,
Because someday
when I'm gone,
they are going to
name that wall after Trump.

September 14, 2015
Trump rally
DALLAS, TEXAS

BAD MAGIC

That's like a magic act.
They send the cars in,
They take our jobs,
They do everything,
And we owe them money.

September 3, 2015
Press briefing
NEW YORK CITY

SIT DOWN, JORGE

Sit down.
You weren't called.
Sit down.
Sit down.
Go ahead.
No, you don't.
You haven't been called.
Go back to Univision.
Go ahead.
Go ahead.
Sit down, please.
You weren't called.

August 25, 2015
News conference
Dubuque, Iowa
CNN *ANDERSON COOPER 360°*

MY WALL

I mean,
It would be,
It would be tall,
It would be powerful,
We would make it very good looking.
It would be as good as a wall's got to be,
And people will not be climbing over that wall.

Believe me.

September 3, 2015
HUGH HEWITT RADIO SHOW

THE RUSSIAN

First of all, you wouldn't want to play
Nuclear weapons with this fucker.
Does he look as tough and cold
As you've ever seen?
This is not like your average real–estate guy
Who's rough and mean.
This guy's beyond that.
You see it in the eyes.
This guy is a killer.

How about when I asked,
Were you a boxer? Whoa!
That nose is a piece of rubber!
But me, he liked.
When we went out to the elevator,
He was grabbing me,
Holding me,
He felt very good.
And he liked what I do.

May 19, 1997
THE NEW YORKER

FRIEND OF VLADIMIR

Putin hates us.
He hates Obama.
He doesn't hate us.
I think he'd like me.

I'd get along great
With him, I think . . .
If you want to
Know the truth.

No, he has no respect
For our president,
And our president
Doesn't like him.

August 29, 2015
*National Federation of Republican
Assemblies*
NASHVILLE, TENNESSEE

MCDONALD'S

Our people don't have a clue.
We give state dinners
To the heads of China.
I said, "Why are you doing

State dinners for them?
They're ripping us left and right.
Just take them to McDonald's,
And go back to the negotiating table."

Seriously.

July 21, 2015
SUN CITY, SOUTH CAROLINA

BORING CHINA

China has declared war on electronic porn.
That means no nudity on the Internet.
No sexy text messages.
No racy radio talk shows.
And no phone sex.
It sounds to me
Like it might be a pretty boring country.

2004
Trumped!
CLEAR CHANNEL PREMIERE
RADIO NETWORKS

WE DON'T GET ALONG

We don't get along with China.
We don't get along with the heads of Mexico.
We don't get along with anybody,
and yet, at the same time,

they rip us left and right.
They take advantage of us
economically and every other way.
We get along with nobody.

I will get along, I think.

September 16, 2015
CNN GOP Presidential Debate
SIMI VALLEY, CALIFORNIA

TO CHINA

Listen, you
Motherfuckers

We're gonna
Tax you
25 percent.

April 28, 2011
Clark County GOP reception
LAS VEGAS, NEVADA

SAUDI

Saudi Arabia.
They make a billion dollars a day.
A billion dollars a day.

I love the Saudis.
Many are in this building.
They make a billion dollars a day.

June 16, 2015
Announcement of presidential candidacy
NEW YORK CITY

FILL 'ER UP

You take the oil.
It's simple.
You take the oil.
There are certain areas
Which ISIS has the oil,
And you take the oil,
You keep it.
You just go in
And take it.

September 3, 2015
THE ECONOMIST

GETTIN' 'EM

Hey! You believe
this goddamn ISIS?

Chopping people's heads off?
Putting people in cages,
and drowning 'em?

We gotta waterboard 'em!
Don't you agree?

September 9, 2015
Rolling Stone
"TRUMP SERIOUSLY: ON
THE TRAIL WITH THE GOP'S
TOUGH GUY"

MUSLIMS

Most are fabulous
And I say that.

Number one point:
Most are fabulous.

September 20, 2015
ABC *THIS WEEK*

ICE

If you want to make ice, you
Call the Canadians,
Right?

I mean, there's nothing wrong
With a little Canadian
Help.

May 27, 2014
NATIONAL PRESS CLUB

PART SIX

'MERICA

AMERICA, WINNER

Nobody's going to mess with us.
Okay? Nobody. And we're going
To have victories, so many victories
That are going to be coming out.

In fact, you might get tired of victories.
You may not want any more.
And everyone stood up and said,
"No, no, no! We want to keep winning!"

If I win, we will have victories all over.
We will win on trade.
We will win on health care.
We will win on everything.

August 29, 2015
National Federation of Republican
Assemblies
NASHVILLE, TENNESSEE

FREEDOM TOWER

    I.
Worst pile of crap
Architecture
I've ever seen.

    II.
The terrorists win.
It's that bad.

May 19, 2005
Press conference
NEW YORK CITY

AWFUL AMERICA

The phones don't work.
They're forty years old.
They have wires that are no good.
Nothing works.
Our country doesn't work.
Everybody wins, except us.

September 3, 2015
Press briefing
NEW YORK CITY

EVERYBODY

This doesn't sound very Conservative:
We've got to take care of everybody,

Not just the people up here.
We've got to take care of everybody.

OK? Get used to it, Conservatives.
I love you, Conservatives. Get used to it.
Let's take care of everybody.

July 11, 2015
PHOENIX, ARIZONA

NOT MY PROBLEM

I would hate to think that people blame me
for the problems of the world.

Yet people come to me and say,
"Why do you allow homelessness in the cities?"

As if I control the situation.
I am not somebody seeking office.

March 1990
PLAYBOY

LOSER PRESIDENTS

I don't want my President
to be carried off a race course.

I don't want my President
landing on Austrian soil
and falling down the stairs of his airplane.

Some of our Presidents
have been incredible jerk-offs.

March 1990
PLAYBOY

JOHN KERRY, SCHMUCK

We have Kerry that goes
On bicycle races.
He's seventy-three years old.
Seventy-three years old!
And I said it the last time I spoke.
I swear I will never
Enter a bicycle race
If I'm president.

I swear, I swear!
He's in a bicycle race.
He falls; he breaks his leg.
This is our chief negotiator.
He is walking in.
They're looking at him like,
"WHAT A SCHMUCK!"

August 25, 2015
Speech in Dubuque, Iowa
CNN *ANDERSON COOPER 360°*

THE LOOMING THREAT

I like George Bush very much
and support him and always will.
But I disagree with him
when he talks of a
"kinder, gentler America."
I think if this country gets any
"kinder or gentler,"
it's literally going to cease to exist.

March 1990

PLAYBOY

DISBELIEF

It's hard to believe
some of the people
that we have
in office.

And then
it's even harder
to believe
some of the people
they appoint.

September 13, 2015
CBS *FACE THE NATION*

CORRECTION

You know the amazing thing?
Every country in the world
Thinks the United States
Is represented by stupid people.
And they're right, of course.

No, they're wrong . . .
VERY stupid people.

August 25, 2015
Trump rally
DUBUQUE, IOWA

NOT CRASS

We got to make
The country rich . . .
It sounds crass.

Somebody said,
"Oh, that's crass!"
It's not crass.

June 16, 2015,
Announcement of presidential candidacy
NEW YORK CITY

REPUBLICANS

I really believe
the Republicans are
just too crazy right.

I mean, just what's going on
is just nuts.

October 26, 1999
NBC *MEET THE PRESS*

I WATCHED THE REPUBLICAN DEBATE LAST NIGHT . . .

I watched the Republican debate last night . . .
And I'll tell you what:

If the right person was debating against
Whoever the winner of that group is,
They'd have a major impact on the election,
Because that was not a very inspiring group.

January 7, 2000
Joint news conference with Jesse Ventura
BROOKLYN PARK, MINNESOTA

BUSH'S FOLLY

Saddam Hussein didn't knock down World Trade
    Center.
He had nothing to do with it.

And there were no weapons of mass destruction.
There was nothing.

Saddam Hussein, you know what he did with the
    terrorists?
He killed them.

He would kill terrorists. And now Iraq is a breeding
    ground.
That's where all the terrorists are going.

They're going to Iraq, because that's the safest place
for them to be.

                              October 15, 2007
                              CNN *LARRY KING LIVE*

HILLARY AND JOHN McCAIN
WERE BIRTHERS

Hillary Clinton was a birther.
She wanted the records
And fought like hell.
People forget.

Do you know,
John McCain was a birther?
Wanted those records.
They couldn't get the records.

Hillary . . . failed!
John McCain . . . failed!
Trump was able to get them
to give *something*!

I don't know what the hell it was.

July 9, 2015
CNN *ANDERSON COOPER 360°*

SOMETHING FISHY
THIS WAY CAME

He gave whatever
it was he gave.

I'm not exactly sure
what he gave,

But he gave
something called

a "birth certificate."

March 24, 2015
FOX NEWS CHANNEL
THE KELLY FILE

WHAT KIND OF GUN DO I HAVE?

I'd rather not say.
I have a gun.
It's a handgun, OK?
It's a gun.
I have a gun.
It's a handgun.

May 11, 2011
ROLLING STONE

CHUMP CHANGE, TRUMP CHANGE

People want to see REAL change,
Not OBAMA change.
He used the word "change."

His change was a BAD change.
They want to see PROPER change.
They want to see GREAT change.

> August 23, 2015
> ABC *THIS WEEK*

NOTHINGNESS

They go to Washington.
They look at the magnificent,
Hallowed halls, as you would say,
Or the beautiful vaulted ceilings,

And they say, "Darling, I've arrived!"
To their loved one or their wife.
They say, "Darling, I've arrived!"
And all of a sudden they become nothing.

They become nothingness.

September 3, 2015
THE ECONOMIST

HELLHOLE AMERICA

The bridges are falling apart.
The roads are falling apart.
The medians are . . .
The airports look like hell.
The airports . . .
I come back from places like Qatar,

    We're doing a tremendous job in Dubai,
    two actually very big jobs in Dubai.
    The airports are unbelievable.

Then we land at LaGuardia.
It's Third-World country.
We land at Kennedy.

Potholes.

May 21, 2015
FOX NEWS CHANNEL
THE KELLY FILE

BAD FUTURE HAIKU

The world is rocky,
And some terrible things are
Going to happen.

October 2004
PLAYBOY

THE JOY OF NOT RUNNING

I'm not running for office.
I don't have to be politically correct.
I don't have to be a nice person.
Like I watch some of these
Weak-kneed politicians,
It's disgusting.
I don't have to be that way.

October 28, 2006
CNN *ANDERSON COOPER 360°*

PART SEVEN

TRUMP 2016

TRUMP, GOOD

I have the right temperament.
I have the right leadership.
I've built an incredible company.
I went to a great school.

I came out, I built an incredible company.
I wrote the number one selling
Business book of all time:
Trump: The Art of the Deal.

I had tremendous success in show business,
Star on the Hollywood Walk of Fame.
The Apprentice was one
Of the most successful shows.

And, as you know, NBC renewed it.

August 20, 2015
TIME INTERVIEW

NICE TO BE NICE

Somebody said . . .
"You win on leadership by far!
You win on absolute economic, financial,
Anything having to do with the economy!
You're like lapping the field!
Much, much higher than anybody else!"
But they said,
"But a lot of people don't know
Whether or not they like you."

I'm actually a nice person.

July 11, 2015
PHOENIX, ARIZONA

OFF THE RECORD

People that were criticizing me two weeks ago
are calling me and they're saying,

> "Off the record,
> Mr. Trump,
> you were right."

And even reporters, a couple of them called—
and they, I said, would you go on the record?

> "No, no, no,
> we don't want
> to do that."

July 21, 2015
SUN CITY, SOUTH CAROLINA

HOLLYWOOD BLACKLIST

I'm friendly with
so many Hollywood people.
They're calling me
and they're saying,
"Donald, I'm a super liberal,
I'm voting for you.
Do me a favor.
Don't tell anybody."

August 19, 2015
HOLLYWOOD REPORTER

APPRECIATING BILL MAHER, DESPITE HAVING BEEN CALLED "NASTY, BORING, SEXIST, IGNORANT" AND "THE SPAWN OF AN ORANGUTAN"

Bill Maher has been,
in a certain way,
very respectful of me.

In fact, a couple of months ago,
before the polls started coming out,
he said, "He's not goin' away!"

Because he's a smart guy.
He gets me.
He *understands*.

August 19, 2015
HOLLYWOOD REPORTER

MORE THAN DOUBLE EVERYBODY

More important than actually,
Literally, killing everybody in the poll.
We were much, much higher,
More than double everybody.
And we are more than double everybody.

August 29, 2015
National Federation of Republican Assemblies
NASHVILLE, TENNESSEE

WHAT KIND OF FOOL AM I?

Nobody's putting up millions of dollars for me.
I'm putting up my own money.
In fact, I feel a little bit foolish.

People are offering me
Millions and millions of dollars.
You know, when you're in first place,

You can collect so much money?
And I keep turning them down.
I feel like: Am I a fool?

September 3, 2015
Press briefing
NEW YORK CITY

OH, THE WINS YOU'LL WIN
(A SEUSSIAN SPIN)

You know what the writer,
the *Times*, told me? He said,

"It's been amazing
What you've done!"

I said, "But . . .
I haven't *WON*!

We haven't won
anything.

What if I won?
I'm having *fun*

and all, but
I haven't WON!"

September 14, 2015
Trump rally
DALLAS, TEXAS

THE PROPHET

My wife didn't even believe me.
But now she does.
But she actually said,

If you actually say
You're going to run,
You're going to do great,
Because people like you.

She actually said,
They'd LOVE you.
But I don't want to brag.

August 29, 2015
National Federation of Republican
Assemblies
NASHVILLE, TENNESSEE

DON'T CALL ME DEBATER

These politicians—
I always say,
they're all talk, no action.
They debate all the time.
They go out
And they debate
Every night.
I don't debate.
I build.
I've created tremendous jobs.
I've built a great company.
I do a lot of things.
And maybe my whole life
Is a debate, in a way.
But the fact is
I'm not a debater.

August 2, 2015
ABC *THIS WEEK*

THE UPCOMING DEBATE

I'm going into a lion's den.
Some people say I will be,
Some people say I won't.
Somebody will attack.

Somebody.

September 12, 2015
News conference
BOONE, IOWA

COMING PREPARED

I'm not saying I'm the perfect person,
but they have liked me a lot.

And I went and spoke largely
in front of evangelicals last night.

And we had a tremendous time.
We had standing ovations,

And they had a lot of fun.
I brought my Bible.

September 20, 2015
NBC *MEET THE PRESS*

VOTERS

I want them to love Trump.
And I want them to know
I'll do a great job.

As far as candidates?
You know, to me,
They're all the same.

September 12, 2015
Trump rally
BOONE, IOWA

FIRST TO BE LAST

The last thing we need
is another Bush.

Now, I made that statement,
Very strongly,

And now everyone says,
The last thing . . .

You know, they copied it.
I'll be accused

Of copying the statement;
That's the bad thing.

But I said it.
I was the one that said it first!

January 24, 2015
Iowa Freedom Summit
DES MOINES, IOWA

OH, THE POLLS YOU'LL READ!
(A SEUSSIAN SCREED)

The poll just came out,
And I'm tied with Jeb Bush.

    And I said,
    "Oh, that's too bad!
    How can I . . .
    be tied with this guy?

He's terrible!"

             July 11, 2015
             PHOENIX, ARIZONA

JEB

Jeb Bush will not be able
To negotiate against China.
Jeb Bush will not be able
To negotiate against Mexico.

Jeb Bush with Mexico said,
People come in! They come in,
It's an act of love, OK?
It's not an act of love.

August 11, 2015
Press conference
BIRCH RUN, MICHIGAN

VERY NICE PEOPLE

Look, I'm fighting some
very nice people.
Very nice.
Even though
I'm leading in the polls,
but they're very nice people.

But they're never going to do anything.

September 15, 2015
USS *Iowa*
LOS ANGELES

DUMBBELLS

This guy, Lindsey Graham,
He calls me a "jackass" this morning.
And I said to myself,
"You know, it's amazing."

He doesn't seem like a very bright guy. OK?
He actually, probably seems to me
Not as bright, honestly, as Rick Perry.

I think Rick Perry is probably
Smarter than Lindsey Graham.
But what do I know?

July 21, 2015
SUN CITY, SOUTH CAROLINA

DUMB AND DUMBER

RICK PERRY!
He put on glasses
So people will think
He's smart!

You have this guy . . .

LINDSEY GRAHAM!
A total lightweight.
We have people
That are stupid.

July 22, 2015
CNN *ANDERSON COOPER 360°*

THE TRUTH ABOUT BEN

I'm a deal-maker.

I will make great deals
for this country.

Ben can't do that.

Ben's a *doctor*.

September 13, 2015
CBS *FACE THE NATION*

NOT BAD IDIOTS

We have dummies, right?
We have dummies.
We have dummies.
We have people that don't have a clue,
And I don't know, you know . . .

Some people say they're bad people.
Well, I don't think they're bad people.
I think they're incompetent people.
A lot of people think they're bad.
I don't think they're bad.

August 21, 2015
SPEECH IN MOBILE, ALABAMA

SCOTT WALKER

He keeps going back to his pollster,
And his pollster says . . .

"Oh! Trump has a good idea!
Oh! Trump has a bad idea!
Oh! No! Wait a minute!
Trump has a good idea!"

These people don't know.

August 23, 2015
ABC *THIS WEEK*

A VERY NICE WOMAN

She's a very nice woman.
She got fired.
She did a terrible job at Hewlett-Packard.

She lost in a landslide.
Other than that,
She's a very nice woman.

August 16, 2015
ABC *THIS WEEK WITH*
GEORGE STEPHANOPOULOS

THE HIDEOUS EXTERIOR
OF CARLY FIORINA

Look at that face!
Would anyone *vote* for that?
Can you imagine that?
The face of our next *president*?

I mean, she's a woman, and
I'm not s'posedta say bad things.
But really, folks, come on!
Are we *serious*?

September 9, 2015
Rolling Stone
"TRUMP SERIOUSLY: ON
THE TRAIL WITH THE GOP'S
TOUGH GUY"

SWEET CARLY

I.

She did a terrible job at Hewlett-Packard.
She did a terrible job at Lucent.
I mean those companies are just a disaster
And she destroyed Hewlett-Packard.

II.

The Compaq computer deal
Was one of the worst deals
Made in business history.
And she destroyed the company
That she was at before then.
I mean she's been terrible.

III.

She's got a good pitter-patter,
But if you listen to her
For more than five minutes straight,
You get a headache.
So I, I am not concerned with Carly.
I hope she does well.

September 20, 2015
ABC *THIS WEEK*

OH, THE THINGS WE'RE TALKING!
(A SEUSSIAN SQUAWKING)

What we are really TALKING ABOUT?

> in my opinion,
> *security!*
> *the military!*

Of which I really know A LOT ABOUT!

I think one of the biggest surprises will be,

> *if I win,*
> *how good I'll be*
> *at national*
> *SECURITY!*

> September 12, 2015
> *News conference*
> BOONE, IOWA

THE SECRET

You don't want to let people know
what you're going to do,
with respect to certain things that happen.
You don't want the other side to know.

I don't want to give you an answer to that.
If I win, and I'm leading in every single poll,
If I win, I don't want people to know
Exactly what I'm going to be doing.

September 3, 2015
HUGH HEWITT RADIO SHOW

IF

If I were a liberal Democrat,
People would say I'm
The super genius of all time.
The super genius of all time.

August 16, 2015
NBC *MEET THE PRESS*

FRANKLY

Frankly,
With what's happening,
Getting to the starting gate,
The best way for the Republicans to win
Is if I win.

September 3, 2015
Press briefing
NEW YORK CITY

PLEDGE OF ALLEGIANCE

I will be totally pledging my allegiance
To the Republican Party
And the Conservative principles
For which it stands . . .
And we will go out,
And we will fight hard,
And we will win, we will win.

September 3, 2015
Press briefing
NEW YORK CITY

THE ART OF THE NOT-SO-GREAT DEAL

I got nothing.

I really got nothing.
The question was,
What did I get
For signing the pledge?

Absolutely nothing.

September 3, 2015
Press briefing
NEW YORK CITY

HEARTFELT PLEA

Again, this isn't bragging.
Normally, I wouldn't say this,
But I need your fricking votes.

Do you understand that?
Do you understand that?
I mean, normally, I wouldn't . . .

August 29, 2015
*National Federation of Republican
Assemblies*
NASHVILLE, TENNESSEE

ACKNOWLEDGMENTS

Aye-yi-yi! Where do I start? OK,
first, I need to thank . . .

Tom Peyer, the legendary comic
book writer (otherwise total loser)
who helped at every step; and

David McCormick, the great agent
and deal maker (I mean, this guy
is big-league big-time); and

David Hirshey, who ran the show
(by the way, the key, is called
"MANAGEMENT!"); and

Kate Lyons and Amy Baker, world-
class women, who did all the work
(I cherish them all); and

Gregg Kulick, a true artist (not like
the ones who throw crap on a wall and
expect you to genuflect); and

Wait, did I leave anybody out? Oh,
yeah: the Bard himself, without
whose words, inspiration, and candidacy,
this book would never have happened.
Thank you, thank you, thank you,
everybody!

Hart Seely
October 1, 2015
Speech to bathroom mirror

ABOUT THE EDITOR

Hart Seely is an award-winning reporter and a popular humorist. His humor and satire have appeared in *The New Yorker*, the *New York Times*, the *Los Angeles Times*, *National Lampoon*, *Slate*, and elsewhere. In addition to editing *Pieces of Intelligence: The Existential Poetry of Donald Rumsfeld* and *O Holy Cow! The Selected Verse of Phil Rizzuto*, Hart has authored and coauthored several other books, including, most recently, his memoir *The Juju Rules: Or, How to Win Ballgames from Your Couch*. He lives in Syracuse.